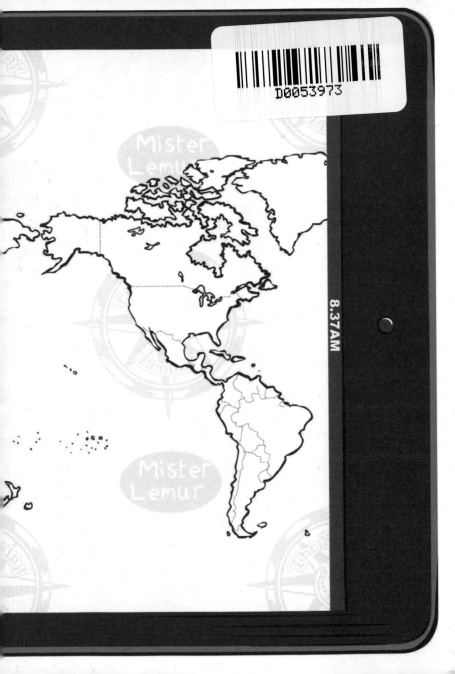

Rivals in Rhyme

RIVALS IN RHYME
By Mister Lemur

Published by
Ringtail Learning,
San Francisco, CA

ISBN: 978-0-9828866-6-3
Library of Congress Control Number: 2014950390

To order, visit www.misterlemur.com. To explore more of
The Scheming Lemurs' world, visit www.TSLband.com

This book is available at a quantity discount when purchased
for educational use. Contact misterlemur@misterlemur.com

Mister Lemur is a trademark of Hans Hartvickson.

Thank you to Mimi Lemur and Amy Bauman for their
editorial insights. A portion of profits from this book will be
donated to causes supporting the protection of lemurs and/or
lemur habitat.

For Annika,

Kids with open eyes and ears will
be amazed at what appears.

RIVALS IN RHYME: MADAGASCAR

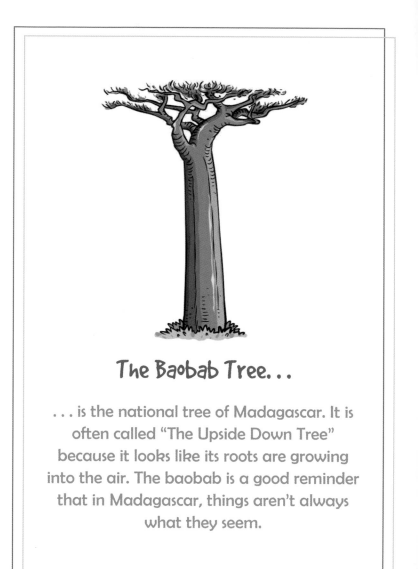

The Baobab Tree...

. . . is the national tree of Madagascar. It is often called "The Upside Down Tree" because it looks like its roots are growing into the air. The baobab is a good reminder that in Madagascar, things aren't always what they seem.

Lemur Notes:

I'm going to start with a confession. Even though the front cover says my name is Mister Lemur. . . my name isn't really Mister Lemur.

Like a lot of writers, I write under a made-up name, called a "pen name." *Mister Lemur* is my pen name. My real name is Oliver. I'm always struggling to be taken seriously as an author because of my age. I think "Mister" makes me sound older.

My parents call me Oliver. My librarian calls me Mister Lemur. My friends sometimes call me Oliver, sometimes call me Mister Lemur, and sometimes call me things I probably shouldn't write in this book. I think of it like my ring tail. Some parts are black, some parts are white, but it's all my tail.

If you have not yet made up a pen name for

yourself, I highly suggest you do.

I also highly suggest you learn to say the word Ranomafana (pronounced RAW Nuh Mah FAW Nuh).

In addition to being cool because it's home to me, a bunch of other lemurs, and my best friend Numbat, *RAW Nuh Mah FAW Nuh* is cool because it's a really fun word to say. Try it.

"Ranomafana"

As we journey together through the pages of this book, you will see that I LOVE to write in rhyme. In fact, I like it so much that I wrote you some rhyming advice about how to read my rhymes.

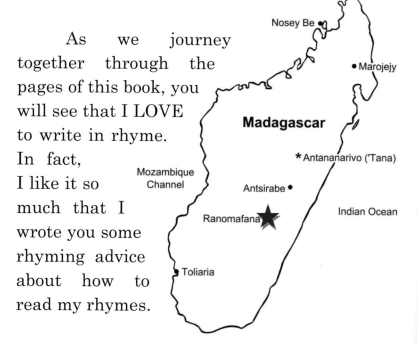

Nosey Be

• Marojejy

Madagascar

★ Antananarivo ('Tana)

Mozambique Channel

Antsirabe •

Ranomafana

Indian Ocean

Toliaria

YOUR BOOK
By Mister Lemur

How should the reader read these rhymes?
I have been asked this many times.

And what I always say to do
is read what brings a smile to YOU.

It is your choice how each will go.
Somemaygofast. Some. . . may. . . go. . . slow.

Speak one like the evening news.
Sing one like you've got the blues.

Read one in a monster's voice.
It is your book. It is your choice!

Disregard! all, punctuation"
Stop to write your own creation.

And if this book stops being fun,
go pick up a different one!

I've also created some videos and songs to help me tell this story. To watch them, you'll need to get on the Internet. I recommend keeping a bookmark nearby so that you can hold your place while you go to a computer or tablet to watch or listen. Don't worry if you don't have Internet access, I created special pages in this book where you can still follow the story even if you are not near the Internet.

SEE ONE OF THESE?

Follow the link online to access music, photos, videos and blogs that accompany the story.

Finally, while I have recorded the events of this story as accurately as I can recall them, in cases where I was not in the room, or was unconscious, I have pieced together parts of the story through interviews, conversations, and the journals of those involved.

I'm very happy you've chosen to come with me on this adventure. If I have calculated correctly, Ranomafana National Park is about half way around the world from your home. That's a LONG trip. . . so without further ado...

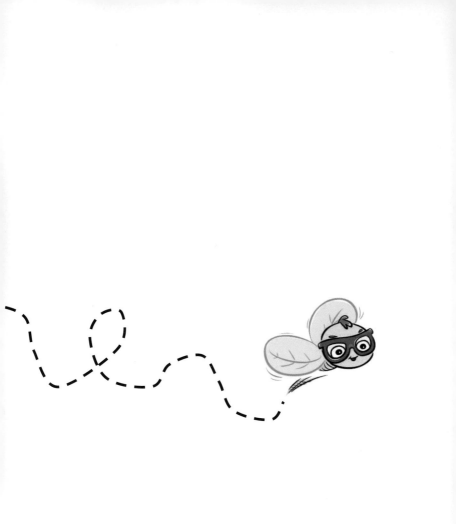

Chapter 1: Muddy Miles

I'm not sure the exact point when night stops and morning begins, but I'm pretty sure I was awake when it happened. I'm also not sure the exact point at which I started to worry that morning, but it was probably around 4:15 a.m. It was raining, there was no sign of Jenny, and there were a lot of muddy miles between me and Madagascar's capital city of Tana.

Finally, I saw a single light approaching up the long dirt path to my house. I was relieved—no question—but I shivered a little at the thought of making the eight-hour drive in the rain with only one of Jenny's headlights working. That seemed pretty unsafe.

As her Jeep got closer, I realized it wasn't a Jeep at all, but... a kid—no, wait... *a numbat*—on a bike.

As Numbat's muddy tires skidded to a halt in front of my house, questions popped into my mind—and out of my mouth—like exploding kernels of popcorn.

"Who? What? Wh—"

"Dude, just grab your bike and follow me. Leave your suitcase," he ordered.

This, of course, prompted about one hundred more questions to pop into my mind, but he sped off, leaving me little choice but to scamper after my own bike or be left behind.

As it was, I had to ride like the wind to keep his bike light from fading off ahead of me into the drizzly, pre—dawn darkness.

NUMBAT

Numbat is a numbat, a type of banded anteater from Southwestern Australia. He used to have a name, but someone actually wore it out, so now people just call him Numbat. That works, since he's the only numbat in Ranomafana National Park.

Chapter 2: Odorous

"This is awful," Jenny moaned.

"This stinks," I added.

"Yeah, it stinks like something that comes out of the south end of a dog going north," Numbat noted, using one of his favorite nicknames for poop.

We all chuckled for the first time that morning.

I reached in my pocket and pulled out a folded flyer.

THE TIME IS NOW

This is YOUR c

RIVALS IN

OPEN
COMPETITION

SATURDAY

January 25th

1:00 PM

at the
Rova complex
in Tana

Rivals in Rhyme is c

NOW IS THE TIME!

nce to be on...

RHYME!

We're looking for the wittiest writers of rhymes, raps, riddles and poems in all of Madagascar. Show off your creativity and talent in front of our judges and a live TV audience. Win prizes! Become famous!

How it works: You and your team will receive a topic and have 60 minutes to craft a rhyme. You will present that rhyme in a battle to be named the most impressive and entertaining rhyme writer in all of Madagascar!

ning to Madagascar!

Rivals in Rhyme is a prestigious international writing contest, with a whole series of rounds that culminate each year in the world championship in some big, far-flung city like London or New York. As far as I can tell, this is the first time they have come to Madagascar to find contestants.

I don't think anyone in elementary school has ever been a contestant on the show before, and I KNOW that no one this young has ever won. . . before.

Numbat and his flashlight emerged from under the hood of Jenny's Jeep.

"Dude, what's particularly odorous about this is that it's not bad luck. This fan belt didn't just break. It was cut. And your spark plugs and radiator are missing. Those don't just fall out.

"We have to find some spare parts or we're not going to make it to Tana."

Odorous (adjective): unpleasant smelling

Chapter 3: Rusted Radiator

The next hour was a frantic burst of creativity. Lemurs don't generally drive cars, so there was no auto parts store in our area of Ranomafana National Park. Instead, Jenny returned with a spark plug from a lawn mower, Numbat found a misshapen radiator from a rusty old tractor, and I talked a security guard in the Centre ValBio research facility into loaning me the belt from his pants.

Our excitement quickly faded when Numbat tried to install them. None of them fit. This was hopeless. We were tired, wet, and frustrated. . . and late.

It was nearly seven, and we had six hours to get someplace that was eight hours away. With heavy hearts, we decided to bike into town to find some hot cider and a dry place to re-group.

Have you ever thought about how dangerous it is for someone with a REALLY long tail to ride a bicycle? A ring-tailed lemur's tail is longer than his body, and. . . I mean. . . I don't even want to think about it!

Chapter 4: Unusual Suspects

As we biked to town, my mind rattled through the list of possible suspects. This wasn't a robbery — nothing valuable was taken. Someone didn't want us to reach the contest.

I know I didn't sabotage the Jeep, and I've known Numbat for years. . .

Lava the Leaf Gecko is a local prankster, but Lava, pranks and all, is usually good natured and harmless...

LAVA THE LEAF GECKO

Leaf geckos get their name from their ability to camouflage themselves to look remarkably like leaves.

Our teammate, Jenny Hart, is probably the most energetic person in all of Ranomafana. She writes books, works in the library, and teaches acting classes. Numbat gets terrible stage fright and I wanted Jenny on the team to help us with the final presentation. . . not to mention that she offered to pick us up at 4:00 a.m. and drive us *eight* full hours to the competition.

Maybe she changed her mind about driving all that way and couldn't bear to tell me? Maybe someone didn't want *her* to go? Maybe she is really bad at auto maintenance?

And then there's Foosana. She is obsessive about becoming a famous singer, and ruthless enough to try to eliminate her competition. But I'm not sure that she even knows about the contest, let alone that Jenny would be driving us. Plus, I don't think she knows enough about how a car works to make one *NOT* work...

Before I could think of any interesting leads, my bald bike tires slid to a stop in front of our favorite hang-out, The Vanilla Bean Café.

Chapter 5: A Furrowed Brow

"The VBC" still had the "closed" sign on the door. Tambo, the old black-and-white ruffed lemur who owns the place, was standing outside looking up at the thick rain clouds with a disapprovingly furrowed brow. His furrowed brow puzzled me, as he always said rain was good for business. When it rains, tourists come inside to get tea and cider and keep dry.

"Can we come in?" I asked. "It's awfully wet out here."

Tambo is very wise, but he has this odd habit of over—emphasizing certain words in a sentence for no reason. It gets even worse when he's excited.

Furrow (verb): to wrinkle one's forehead due to worry or concern

"Aren't you SUPPOSED to be driving to Tana THIS morning?" Tambo furrowed his lemur brow even further and scratched his bushy white beard.

"We're not going to make it." I said, sadly. Then I launched into the whole story.

When we got to the part where the Jeep had been sabotaged, Tambo's mouth hung open in disbelief and he accidently dropped his suitcase right in a mud puddle. I hadn't even realized he was holding a suitcase.

"Who do you THINK. . ." Tambo started, then stopped himself.

Before anyone else could speak, Tambo continued, "OK—so I HAVEN'T been totally honest WITH you."

We all looked at each other.

"Wait—WHAT!?!" Numbat burst out.

I'd never suspected Tambo.

He continued, "The reason you FOUND the flyer for Rivals in Rhyme Madagascar in the VBC is that I'm ONE of the judges. I didn't WANT to tempt you to ask me questions I SHOULDN'T answer, and I didn't want anyone TO think I'm giving you SPECIAL treatment. So I didn't TELL you I was involved.

"I'm about to CATCH a ride with Baron Von Blake on his mail FLIGHT to Tana. It's awful that someone SABOTAGED your Jeep. If there is room on THE plane, you should COME with us. Flying is THE only way you'll MAKE it on time."

We looked at Tambo. He looked to the sky. "That is—if any OF us make it ON time. This storm looks pretty nasty."

TAMBO

A retired author and songwriter, he was given the nickname "Tambo" because of his skill playing the tambourine. This black-and-white ruffed lemur is one of the main supporters of live local music in Ranomafana.

Chapter 6: The Baron

We waited inside The VBC until a rickety 'ol pickup pulled into the muddy parking lot. The driver, clad in knee-high rubber galoshes, collected the mail from a large metal box marked "La Poste." He then slung the canvas sack over one of his burly shoulders.

Tambo warned us there was a good chance The Baron wouldn't have room.

"SQWEEEEEEKKKK... WHACK!"

The Baron entered The VBC, letting the screen door slam shut behind him.

Tambo met him at the door. After some pleasantries, they began talking quietly, out of ear-shot. They talked for a long time. Each

Burly (adjective): strongly and heavily built

time The Baron nodded his head in a "yes" motion our emotions would leap, only to be replaced by despair every time he shook his head "no." What if he could only take one of us? Two of us? Who would go?

I looked away and took a deep breath to calm myself. When I looked back, The Baron was walking toward us. His galoshes left muddy footprints on The VBC's wooden floor with each step he took.

In a booming, noticeably fake French accent, he began, **"I sink eat ees terrib–leh, zees bees–niece weeth zee Zheep."**

In a town full of characters, Baron Von Blake might be the most unusual. As the story goes, his great, great, great grandfather held several very important positions with the government when Madagascar was a French colony. This was a long time ago– Madagascar was a French colony from 1897 to 1960. He claims that

this great, great, great grandfather was French nobility, and that this lineage—this family history—makes him a baron.

Tambo once told me that "Baron Von Blake" actually has an Australian passport saying "Blake" is his first name and "Vaughn" is his last name.

He also claims to have a pet enchilada, but that doesn't even make sense. It's rumored that his favorite food is pickle pancakes.

The only thing we know for sure is that "The Baron" has a good imagination.

And a really bad accent.

Anyway, he proceeded to tell us that while his plane was very full of important mail, we were very lucky because he was the best pilot in all of Madagascar. He could get us there safely. All of us.

We hoped he wasn't making up that last part.

Chapter 7: Par Avion

We had to pack and re-pack the plane three times to get everything (and everyone) to fit. Then we sat on the plane and waited.

The low clouds and lack of visibility made it too dangerous to take off right away. 8:30. . . 8:45. . . 9:00 passed. That familiar "We're not going to make it" feeling crept back into my stomach.

Since we had nothing else to do, I suggested that we practice for the competition. That is when I realized that winning this contest might not be as easy as I had thought.

According to the Rivals in Rhyme flyer, contestants have sixty minutes to write a rhyming story and prepare a presentation for the judges and the audience. As we practiced, it took us sixty minutes just to get everyone to agree on the topic and, maybe–if we were lucky–the rhyme scheme.

Everyone had different opinions on everything. It seemed that Numbat's attention span was about five seconds long. Every time we'd start to get serious about an idea, he'd interject, "Dudes! Wait! I got it! What about _____ instead?" and totally derail the conversation. With every idea, I found myself skeptically thinking, "How are we actually going to *present* that?!"

After a frustrating hour, I frustratedly exclaimed, "I'm frustrated. Maybe working as a team was NOT such a good idea."

Tambo looked up from his book. "Oliver, you are really good AT puzzles, right? Putting TOGETHER a team is a lot like PUTTING together a puzzle. You need different pieces THAT all fit together THE right way. Some pieces HAVE just blue sky or WATER, and they don't seem that important, WHILE others have all THE action. But you NEED all

19

the right pieces IN all the right places to MAKE the team work."

He continued, "Remember that STORY about puzzles THAT you wrote? Think ABOUT that story, and you'll FIND the key TO your team."

Without saying another word, Tambo put his muzzle back into his book.

I was puzzled. I flipped through my notebook and found a story I had written at Adventures in Writing Camp the summer before. It's called "Puzzled." I began reading it aloud.

TSLband.com/RR21

- Once you have finished watching the video, skip to page 24.
- If you do NOT have access to the Internet, turn the page and continue reading.

Puzzled
By Mister Lemur

I puzzled and puzzled and
I puzzled all over the walls
I puzzled for hours. I puzzl
I puzzled in bed despite al

I puzzled with cousins and
I puzzled a puzzle with te
I puzzled in blindfolds so
there's no one who puzzles

But now I am puzzled. I h
I am missing one piece. I
I have reached to look hig
But this piece has no legs.

It's so close to completion
but I'm puzzled where I'll

zled some more.
d the floor.
hrough meals.
m's appeals.

les and nieces.
usand pieces.
le could see
deftly as me!

't a clue.
t know what to do!
ave stooped to look low.
ean, where could it go?

n't want to cease…
that one missing

Deftly (adjective): quickly and accurately
Cease (verb): to stop

When I finished reading, everyone was silent. Even the rain had stopped falling.

Then Numbat practically fell off his stack of mail.

"Dudes! Do you know what would be sweet? What if we got Silky—the music producer—to join our team? He's the best producer and DJ in Ranomafana; you know what I'm saying? And he is a really talented musician and songwriter."

Jenny and I just stared at Numbat, processing his sudden, over-the-top enthusiasm. We'd never met Silky. And—hopefully—we were going to be taking off for Tana at any moment.

"Think about it! Right? As a music producer, he's good at taking people with crazy different skills and talents and getting them to work together to sound totally rad. When we write our rhymes, we have to choose a meter—a rhythmic structure—for the words. That meter is like the rhythm or beat of a song. Silky has an

---

Producer (noun): Someone responsible for the recording of music

amazing ear for meter and rhythm... and that's huge for us. You know what I'm saying?"

Jenny slowly nodded. She *did* know what he was saying. "You're right! We need Silky—he's our missing piece!"

As soon as the words "missing piece" were out of Jenny's mouth, it hit me. Tambo was right. We were still short of a complete puzzle, and Silky, if he would join, was our one missing

piece.

Numbat convinced The Baron to hold the plane, and then he set out into the forest to find Silky's studio. I wondered if Silky would accept. I wondered if this would still be "my team" if he did. Was it still "my" team anyway?

Meter (noun): A pattern of beats per line in a song or poem

Chapter 9: Potholes

Finally, at nearly 10:30, with Silky and his considerable baggage aboard, The Baron fired up the engines, and we began to taxi. Our "seats" on the plane were under, behind, and (mostly) on sacks of mail and bundles of postcards.

 I could see Silky studying me intently from across the plane. I felt him thinking, "THIS is the great author Numbat told me about? He's just a kid. Is this a joke?" At least, that's what I thought he was thinking.

The long takeoff in the overloaded plane was a nail–biter, but soon we were airborne, circling over the cloudy park and heading northeast. It was not exactly riding in style, but it was riding.

Our time in flight did nothing to change the idea that The Baron had quite the imagination. To keep myself calm during the second half of the trip—and to get warmed up for the competition—I drafted this poem:

POTHOLES
By Mister Lemur

The flight to Tana rocked and rolled us.
"A summer storm," Jenny told us.
Then Silky started freaking out.
"Stop the plane! I'm getting out!"

The Baron yelled, "I can explain!"
as mail bounced around the plane.
"This stretch of sky's in disrepair!
You see those potholes in the air?"

I didn't have the heart to say,
"I don't think flying works that way."
And so I said, "Of course I do!
We're going to need a maintenance crew!"

"We'll need a crew that can repave.
A crew that's light. A crew that's brave.
A crew that's skilled. A crew that's shrewd
enough to pave at altitude."

But as Sir Isaac Newton knows
the sky's a hard thing to bulldoze.
And no one's made a sky–road base
that has been shown to stay in place.

So next time that you wonder why
you're hitting potholes in the sky
don't curse your local D–O–T,
just know that's how it's gonna be.

'Cause 'till there's asphalt light as air
the sky will stay in disrepair!

D–O–T: Department of Transportation (noun): the part of the
government that typically builds and repairs roads

Hmm. "Funny concept, but not my best work," I thought, as I re-read my poem. "I rhymed *us* with *us* and *out* with *out* in the first stanza. That's the kind of lyrical cop-out the judges won't appreciate." I stuffed my notebook and pencil back into the pocket of my overalls, wrapped my tail around my head and pretended to sleep. I was no longer feeling confident about our ability to win this contest.

Chapter 10: Antananarivo (Tana)

The full name of Madagascar's capital city is actually Antananarivo ("On–TAH–Nuh–Nuh–REEVE–Oh), but most people just call it Tana (TAH–Nuh) for short.

We touched down at Tana's Ivato (ih–VAH–toe) airport–hitting an actual pothole on the landing strip–fewer than thirty minutes from the start of the contest. The Baron had radioed ahead to the airport to have a taxi waiting for us, and–in a sign that perhaps our luck was improving–a taxi was indeed waiting for us when we landed.

The cab was small, and its trunk was stuck closed, so we piled everyone and everything into the back seat. Soon we were racing along one of Tana's many winding, crowded streets. We sat quietly, nervously watching the clock on the cab's dashboard and trying not to get carsick.

Tambo finally broke the silence, addressing a question no one had asked. "YOU KNOW, you aren't the only TEAM from RANOMAFANA. Foosana and a few of her FRIENDS are also COMPETING in today's contest. I knew Foosana's dad WHEN I was younger. His NAME was Snarlton, and he was a very, very GOOD singer. I wrote the lyrics TO a few songs for him. He was always traveling AROUND from village to village playing music, trying to GET his big break. As talented AS Snarlton was, he never HAD much success. He was never well known OUTSIDE the southern villages.

"It's a PITY though. Because her parents WERE gone so much, Foosana didn't get enough ATTENTION growing up. I think she really wants to win this CONTEST to become an international sensation. She knows if she DOES that, she will get attention FROM everyone." Tambo paused, sighing deeply. "And she WILL achieve what her DAD never coul–"

 **Bang!**

The taxi driver slammed on his breaks. We–and our bags–were thrown into the seats in front of us. Silky screamed. We'd nearly crashed into a team of Zebu cattle that had dropped its cargo in the street.

No one was injured, but we were all a little shaken. This cab ride was making our flight with The Baron seem relaxing. Eventually we made it to the Rova complex—with just minutes to spare.

Chapter 11: The Rova Complex

When I got to the check-in desk, the concerned woman asked, "Are you looking for your parents?" She raised an eyebrow when I told her I was entering a team... but handed me the entry forms anyway.

We hurriedly choose the name "Mister Lemur and The Scheming Lemurs." Tambo had jokingly referred to us as "you scheming lemurs" the night before as we sat whispering and planning in The VBC. I liked the name. I thought it made us sound mischievous.

Each contestant was required to present a valid identification showing they were a resident of Madagascar. The nice woman didn't have time to complete our paperwork and check our identification, so she told us to go ahead inside, and to come back after round one. . . if we advanced to round two. Judging

Mischievous (adjective): causing trouble in a fun way

by the smirk on her face, I don't think she thought there was much chance we'd advance.

We were in our seats in a building in the Rova complex (the royal palace) *maybe* sixty seconds before the contest began. I looked around. I didn't see any TV cameras. Other than a few family members, virtually no one was in the audience. I frowned.

What I did see was Foosana's team in the front row. It included Lava and two of the musicians from her band. They were registered as "Miss Foosa." Foosana must have felt my eyes on her. She turned around and looked surprised for just a moment before smiling and waving to us.

A short, round–faced man named Parson stepped to the podium and addressed the participants.

Parson welcomed us, and, in a very calm and measured voice, explained the rules.

"YOU WILL RECEIVE A TOPIC AND HAVE SIXTY MINUTES TO PREPARE A POEM OR RHYMING STORY,

AS WELL AS A PRESENTATION, FOR THE PANEL OF
JUDGES.

"YOU CAN'T RE-USE A TOPIC. EACH JUDGE
WILL SCORE EACH TEAM ON A SCALE OF ONE
THROUGH TEN. THEY GIVE POINTS FOR
ENTERTAINMENT VALUE, WIT, RHYME SCHEME, AND
PRESENTATION. THE AVERAGE SCORE GIVEN BY THE
JUDGES IS THE TEAM'S SCORE."

There were seventeen teams
participating. The top eight would advance to
the second round later this afternoon.

Parson fielded a few questions from the
captains and told each team where their
"workshop" space was located. He then pulled
out a sealed envelope and dramatically read,

"THE TOPIC FOR THE FIRST ROUND IS. . ."

Chapter 12: Animals

"Animals? Just animals, with no other details?" **Silky** wrinkled his nose as he spoke. *"That seems really vague."* Silky, Jenny, Numbat, and I, along with the other teams, were being shuffled through a long corridor that led to our private work spaces.

As soon as the door to our workshop closed behind us and we were alone, everyone spoke at once. *"Dogs!"* *"Everyone loves dogs!"* Numbat pointed out that everyone loves kangaroos too, but Silky noted that might just be in Australia. Numbat was outvoted.

We bounced around a few sappy dog poem concepts before it hit me. I had been through a comically frustrating experience bringing my dog Henry to field day about a year ago. The team loved it. That experience became. . .

I BROUGHT MY DOG
TO FIELD DAY
By Mister Lemur

When we picked teams for field day
my dog was drafted first.
At times he was the best one there.
At times he was the worst.

Though Henry's quite a nimble dog,
it would have made more sense
to keep him on the sidelines for
the more complex events.

While Henry's great at running sprints,
we finished in last place
(in a barking heap of grass-stains)
in our first three-legged race.

"Three legs" is hard with just one dog
but when you add his master,
and bind them for a three-leg sprint?
Unparalleled disaster!

We bound our legs for three more tries,
(each time a new arrangement).
But every time we'd trip and fall
we'd deepen our estrangement.

A dog may be a man's best friend,
but dogs are not designed
to be racing right beside us
while our legs are intertwined.

"I Brought My Dog to Field Day" was a hit with the judges. They laughed out loud as we acted out the failed three-legged race attempts. Jenny played the part of the kid, and I tied Silky—who was walking on all fours—to her leg with the belt I'd forgotten to return to the security guard that morning. I hoped he knew his pants had been falling down all day for a good reason.

Estrangement (noun): no longer being on friendly terms
Intertwined (verb): twisted together

Chapter 13:
It's All Fun and Games Until. . .

We celebrated when the judges announced "The Scheming Lemurs" as the top overall score in the first round. We'd scored a 9.8 out of a possible 10. Silky was impressed, and I'm pretty sure that he stopped caring about my age. Numbat's stage fright had kicked in right before the skit, but there were really only two roles, so it wasn't a problem that he didn't participate. The eight remaining teams included Miss Foosa, who finished third with a poem about birds.

Parson reminded us that the top four teams in the second round would advance to tomorrow's finals, and then he released us for a thirty-minute break. We went back to the front desk to finish signing in. When we were done, the woman accidentally handed me

Silky's passport. Not knowing Silky very well, I was curious to learn more. I flipped open the cover and glanced inside.

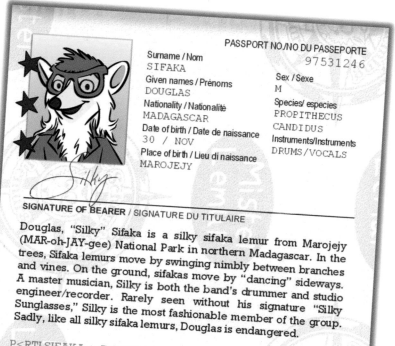

PASSPORT NO./NO DU PASSEPORTE
97531246

Surname / Nom
SIFAKA

Given names / Prénoms
DOUGLAS

Nationality / Nationalité
MADAGASCAR

Date of birth / Date de naissance
30 / NOV

Place of birth / Lieu di naissance
MAROJEJY

Sex / Sexe
M

Species/ especies
PROPITHECUS
CANDIDUS

Instruments/Instruments
DRUMS/VOCALS

SIGNATURE OF BEARER / SIGNATURE DU TITULAIRE

Douglas, "Silky" Sifaka is a silky sifaka lemur from Marojejy (MAR-oh-JAY-gee) National Park in northern Madagascar. In the trees, Sifaka lemurs move by swinging nimbly between branches and vines. On the ground, sifakas move by "dancing" sideways. A master musician, Silky is both the band's drummer and studio engineer/recorder. Rarely seen without his signature "Silky Sunglasses," Silky is the most fashionable member of the group. Sadly, like all silky sifaka lemurs, Douglas is endangered.

P<RTLSIFAKA<<DOUGLAS<<<<<<<<<<<<<<<<<<<<<<<
97531246RTL201009171M1006113<<<<<<<<<<<<<<<

Nimbly (adjective): moving with ease

Did you read the part of his passport that says "On the ground, sifakas move by 'dancing' sideways?" It's true. In the short time I've known Silky, any time he moves from one place to another, he moves by dancing his way there. He danced his way to the Baron's plane. He danced his way to the taxi. He even danced his way to the Rova complex to begin the competition! I like watching Silky move about. So much so, that I even took a short video of him.

TSLband. com/RR44

That may sound funny, but I've tried it. I tried it when no one was looking, of course, but I still tried it. And you know what? It's hard to be in a bad mood when you go through your day dancing from place to place. I highly suggest you try it sometime, too.

Another thing about Silky that took some getting used to is his sense of style. He is rarely seen without his signature orange "Silky Sunglasses," and he is REALLY into looking good.

That is a little odd for me, since I wear blue overalls. Every. Single. Day.

However, as Tambo says, "The clothes don't make THE man, but no one really knows what makes THE lemur." So maybe Silky's onto something.

Chapter 14: Games

"Dude—these are pretty generic topics," Numbat noted when "games" was announced as the second-round topic.

Once again turning to my family for inspiration, I thought of a game I like to play with my dog. It's almost more of a social experiment. I follow my dog around and do what he does. I "emulate" him.

We were feeling a lot of momentum for dog stories after the first round, and after I quickly came up with a few stanzas, the team was hooked. Silky was working well as the "music producer" of the group, and our meter was smooth and consistent.

Thirty minutes into the sixty minute prep time, we had finished the poem.

Generic (adjective): having no particularly distinctive quality

EMULATE
By Mister Lemur

In the dog days of August,
I've been known to play,
a new game that will help me
see dogs a new way.

This new game is not hard.
It has one main directive.
. . . you must look at the world
from a puppy's perspective.

From the time I wake up,
'til I curl in my bed,
"I'm a dog! I'm a dog!"
will repeat in my head.

I'll eat all of my meals
from a bowl on the floor.
I will enter the house
through a small doggie door.

When I need to speak up,
I'll speak only in bark.
I'll do all of my "business"
on grass in the park.

Ok, maybe not that,
since my father suggested
doing *that* in the park
just might get me arrested!

I will shake. I will dig.
I'll uproot plants and trees.
And I'll keep my paws crossed
I don't get ticks or fleas.

I will do the dog paddle
each time that I swim.
I will follow my dog
and I'll emulate him.

Emulate (verb): to mimic or copy the actions of another

As I go through my day
I'll be certain to choose
to live life like I'm walking
ten miles in his shoes.

When I emulate him
it's just one of the ways
that I like to have fun
in the August dog days.

Jenny and I were cracking ourselves up over how to act out the "do all of my 'business' on grass in the park" line when Silky started screaming.

Seriously. He just dance–ran around the room–screaming.

"Aaaagghhhhhh!! Aaaagghhhhhh!! Aaaaagghhhhhh!!"

We were all too shocked to say anything, except Numbat, who got out the word "Dude." It wasn't clear which of the many meanings of "dude" he intended, but it was probably several all at once.

On his third screaming lap around the room, Silky changed course and ran right at us. He grabbed the poem and began shredding it into tiny pieces. Then—to our horror—he began eating the pieces. Within seconds the poem was gone.

Numbat tackled Silky, and the two wrestled for a moment before the country-strong Numbat pinned the skinny, hyperventilating sifaka lemur.

Jenny spoke first. "Are. . . are you okay? What HAPPENED?!"

We had just over twenty minutes left on the clock.

Silky gasped, *"I just re-read the rules. We can't use the same topic twice. We wrote a story about dogs in the first round. If we write a story about dogs in this round, we'll be disqualifaaaaaagggghhh."* He broke into hysterics again as soon as the word *disqualified* began to come out of his mouth.

I ran to the rulebook and furiously read the instructions. It wasn't clear. Was "dogs" our topic in round one, or was it the more specific "a dog at field day?" If we wrote a story about a dog doing a different event–say, the pole vault–at field day, would that be considered a new topic?

This was bad. Our workshop was at the end of a long hallway on the other side of the grounds from the judges. Going to ask them would use up precious time. . . especially if Silky was right.

I took charge, yelling to be heard over Silky's continuing freak out. "It's too risky. We need to think of a new poem that has nothing to do with dogs!"

When I said that, Silky stopped screaming and lay on the ground, exhausted. Numbat grabbed Silky's arm and checked his designer watch. "We have sixteen minutes."

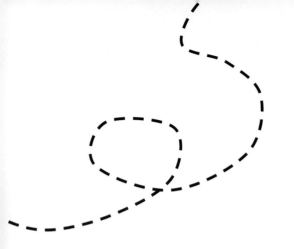

We all started talking as fast as we could about our favorite games. Bowling was the first game that we all agreed we liked.

Silky pulled himself together–sort of–and joined us at the table. But his suggestions were nonsensical. Actually, they were not just nonsensical, they were distractingly bad.

"Dude, can you, like, stand over there please?" Numbat snapped impatiently. "We're trying to DO this." That put Silky into a whimpering, knee-clenching ball in the corner. We'd have to deal with that later.

We threw together a story about bowling in odd shoes. It needed more editing, and none of us were that proud of it. The meter was a little clunky, too. We found that we really missed Silky's input on the meter.

FOOT FAULT
By Mister Lemur

After hours of cajoling,
I said, "Fine! I will go bowling,
but only if I get to choose
the things we wear for bowling shoes."

My friends reluctantly said, "Yes"
but from my rule, they all could guess
that soon, our group would all compete
with odd contraptions on our feet.

I asked the size that each friend wears,
and then I found all kinds of pairs.

In our first frame, right off the bat,
my choice of footwear showed us that
a bowling alley owner hates
when people bowl in roller skates.

Cajoling (verb): Trying to convince someone to do something by
repeated coaxing or flattery

And then, with each successive turn,
through slips and trips and falls, we'd learn

. . . that. . .

if you're forced to bowl in skis
bowl "granny" style, between your knees.

And if you are a knight who owns
some shoes of armor (sabatons)
be conscious of their toe design. . .
stay well behind the foot–fault line.

In our last frame, I chose to wear
two shoes that made a mismatched pair.
One foot wore a small glass slipper.
One foot wore a snorkel flipper!

Successive (adjective): following each other without interruption
Sabaton (noun): A part of a knight's armor that covers the foot

Our bowling scores were all quite poor.
Our feet got blisters. They were sore.
The alley says we can't come back.
The lane we bowled now has a crack.

We put ten shoe types to the test.
So which one did I like the best?
The sabatons, they're made of steel.
They make it certain I won't feel
the slightest bit of pain at all
next time I drop my bowling ball!

As we ran down the hallway to submit our story, Jenny yelled, "We'll 'improv' the presentation. It will be great. Just be silly and follow my lead."

Jenny and I did a decent improvised skit of slipping and falling while bowling in funny shoes. Silky was still trying to get himself together, and he didn't come on stage. Numbat, who hates performing without a script, opted out as well.

As luck would have it, two of the eight remaining teams failed to submit their poems before the sixty minute bell rang. They were disqualified. One of the other groups had messed up their presentation, leaving only five teams competing seriously for the four spots in the final round. Foosana and her gang finished in second place. We squeaked into fourth place by a fraction of a point. Disaster had been averted, and we were going to the finals.

But we sure weren't going there with much momentum.

Chapter 16: Alone

"Let's grab some dinner!" Jenny Hart suggested.

Silky, who had finally chilled out after his freak out, was the lone holdout.

"That sounds like fun," he said unconvincingly, *"but I want to go check out some record shops and hear some live jams."* Then, before any of us could speak, he danced out the door and into the big city.

Alone.

My shoulders fell. It seemed like our team chemistry was crumbling. On top of that, I was frustrated, and my confidence was at an all-time low. Going into this, I was SURE I was the best. I was beginning to think I had overestimated myself.

I sighed and turned to Jenny and Numbat, "I'm going out, too. I'll see you at breakfast."

Sometimes you just need a little time alone.

Chapter 17: The Writing Fly

Although the sun was beginning to set, the streets of Tana still buzzed with shopkeepers, carts, and pedestrians. A woman passed with a head–load of honey jars. Vendors sat under shade umbrellas selling fritters and vegetables and bags of rice. The smell of warm banana bread from a small bakery made my mouth water.

I didn't have my wallet, but I found a small ariary coin in my overalls pocket. The ariary (pronounced by quickly saying the letters "R,e, R,e") is our currency–our "dollar"– in Madagascar. I had just enough ariary for a small slice, and I sat down for a snack.

A peculiar individual was seated next to me on a concrete block. As we ate, we had a most unusual–and fortunate–conversation.

After he left, I pulled out my pocket journal
and wrote this poem.

THE WRITING FLY
By Mister Lemur

Tonight I met a thoughtful guy
who said, "I am the Writing Fly.
In case you've never heard of me,
I'm cousins with the Spelling Bee.
The Spelling Bee's the spelling king,
but helping writers is my thing."

I said, "So if this story's true,
how come I've never heard of you?"

The fly sighed once. He then replied,
"It is a role I've tried to hide.
I'm very shy. I work alone.
I want my deeds to stay unknown.
But since you asked and were polite
I'll tell you all about my flight.

"I will sneak up beside your ear
and whisper things you can't quite hear.
Then I'll buzz off, and you will find
a new idea in your mind.

"I've worked this way for years and years,
but kids today have crowded ears.
If there are ear buds in the way
. . . what's the point? I fly away.

**"But kids with open eyes and ears
will be amazed at what appears."**

So then I said, "What can I do?
I like to help young writers too!"

The fly then rose to fly away.
But as he left, he paused to say,
"Well, yes, here's something you can do.
Let inspiration come to you. . .

**'Cause kids with open eyes and ears
will be amazed at what appears."**

Chapter 18: D.I.Y. Rhymes

Silky didn't actually go out to visit record stores or to hear live music. He would do both that night, but that wasn't the reason he wanted to be alone.

He set off "dance-walking," as sifaka lemurs do, through the big, bustling city, processing everything that had happened during the long, confusing day. He dance-walked with his DJ headphones on his ears. No music was coming through them, but he knew headphones were a good way to keep people from talking to him. Well, some people.

"Step right up to my stall!
I've a deal for you!
I've a deal you'll think
is too good to be true!"

A small chameleon with a booming voice caught Silky's attention amongst the din.

"For the next sixty seconds
(that's a limited time)
I will make you a deal
on a D.I.Y. _____!"

Silky hesitated.

". . . Microwave?"

The chameleon continued:

I will give you the structure
and start off a phrase,
and you'll be free to finish
it all sorts of ways.

I will start off the stories.
You'll be the completer.
You will add words that work
with my rhyme and my _____.

"Rhythm?" Silky exclaimed a little more confidently. He thought he was getting the hang of this.

The chameleon rolled his eyes all the way back in his head. He made a face like he'd just bit into a particularly tart lemon. Then he continued.

You will add rhyming words
to my reptile flow.
A new story is starting.
Let's see where we ___!

"End up!" Silky yelled, nearly jumping as he said it.

"Errrggh. End up somewhere else, pal. Put three thousand ariary in the bowl and beat it." The chameleon spat, turning his attention to a more promising pedestrian.

Silky looked at the chameleon–both shocked and offended–and turned to dance away.

As soon as he started to go, two men stepped out of the shadows and moved toward him purposefully. They were not big men, as men go, but compared to a sifaka lemur they were big enough. He felt a freak out coming. This happened every time he was endangered.

Silky quickly reached in the pocket of his stylish orange shirt and grabbed for his money clip. He sensed he was endangered, and he wanted to get away before he caused a scene. Three thousand ariary was unfair, but smaller than the number of digits might suggest. Just a couple dollars. He was here to get over a freak out–not have another one.

In a rising panic, Silky began frisking himself–checking all his pockets–and found them all empty. He had left his money clip—and all of his money—in his hotel room.

"Aaaagghhhhhh!! Aaaagghhhhhh!! Aaaaagghhhhhh!!"

Passers-by looked. Some stopped to stare, but no one stopped to help.

Chapter 19: A Flying Sleep

Although neither Silky nor I realized it, our evening walks had taken us on similar paths. While he was being shaken down, I was looking at wood carvings just blocks away, trying to let inspiration come to me.

Over the din of the crowd, I heard the now-familiar high-pitched sounds of Silky "losing it." I couldn't tell the exact source of the sound, but I knew it was close.

The square around me was jammed with bargaining shoppers and strolling families. I tried to run toward the sound, but I could barely move through the pedestrian-choked street.

Then, suddenly—TOO suddenly—the sound stopped.

Din (noun): a loud, confusing mixture of noises that lasts for a long time

I held my breath, listening. Ten seconds passed. Nothing.

In a quick, fluid, motion, I sprang onto the shoulders of a man in front of me. I jumped from the top of one head to the next, leaping above the crowd as though I were fleeing from a fossa in the tree-tops. Not everyone appreciated my route, but within seconds, I had crowd-surfed onto a roof near the sound's source.

When I arrived, the two men were carrying Silky towards an alley behind the chameleon's booth. A piece of duct tape covered his mouth.

"Sheesh" I thought. "Silky wasn't kidding. . . he really is an endangered species."

I didn't have much time to think. I shimmied down the side of a building until I was face to face with the lizard.

He began again with the same sales pitch.

Fossa (noun): A slender long-tailed carnivorous mammal that has claws and is found in Madagascar. Sometimes spelled "Foosa"

"Step right up to my stall!
I've a deal for you!
I've a deal you'll think
is too good to be true!"

Before he could get any further, I blurted
out in my loudest, non-yelling voice, "What's
your deal?"

He smiled. *"I'm the best poet in all of Madagascar. For only three thousand ariary I'll help you write a poem! For the next sixty sec. . ."* I cut him off.

"Hold up. . ." I looked at the sign above his booth. ". . . Ponce. . . If you really are the best poet in all of Madagascar, why have I never heard of you?"

"You've never heard of me?" He laughed, making it clear to all within earshot that my claim was ridiculous. *"My great, great, great, great, great, great, great, great, great—"*

"Ok, I get it."

"—grand–lizard used to catch flies for Ponce de León in the early sixteenth century. I am Ponce de Cammie-León."

I realized this Ponce's ego—or his act—was my opportunity.

"Ponce de Cammie-Leon. . . if you think you are the best poet in all of Madagascar, then I've got a deal for YOU!" I said it as loudly as I could, so everyone around us could hear.

Ponce tilted his head to one side, like a dog that was listening. Then he shrugged his shoulders and wrinkled his forehead as if to say, "Well, whadda ya got?"

"You and I have a rhyme battle right here, right now. If you win, I'll give you twenty thousand ariary. If I win, you let that silky lemur go unharmed."

I gestured towards Silky and the two men holding him.

It's hard to con a con-man, or a con-lizard. Ponce hesitated. He had been in this underground world long enough to be suspicious. But, by now, I had the attention of the two men holding Silky. They stopped to watch. So did several passers–by. Ponce's reputation, or at least his ego, wouldn't let him back down.

I began,

"I'll start a story with a phrase.

You add lines two and three.
Then we will alternate our lines,
two you and then two me.

We'll know the contest has been won,
and one of us is trumped,
when one of us can't play our turn
because we have been stumped."

Ponce de Cammie-León turned one of his eyes to look at me, and his other eye to look at the gathering crowd. *"Prepare to be embarrassed, lemur!"*

I started quickly to set the flow:

"I jumped down from a tree stump
with a mighty flying leap. . . "

Ponce responded, completing the first couplet and starting the next:

*". . . but 'soon as I went airborne
my left foot fell fast asleep.*

I thought, "Before I hit the ground
my left foot will awaken."

"But as my left foot touched the ground,
I knew I was mistaken.
The foot was still quite fast asleep,
and it would bear no weight,"

"and so, I fell into my bike, which. . .

Ponce paused and closed his eyes. The crowd gasped for a moment. Was it really going to be this easy? Then he continued,

". . . started off a spate
of poorly timed 'cause and effect',
a messy chain reaction."

"And there was nothing I could do
but sit and watch the action.
My falling bike disturbed a squirrel,
who then disturbed a dog. . . "

Spate (noun): A large number of similar things or events appearing or occurring in quick succession

78

". . . who had been resting peacefully
against a fallen log.
The log then started rolling,
gaining steam on down the hill. ."

"It rolled and rolled and rolled and rolled and
rolled and rolled until
the log crashed right into our house.
It nearly felled a wall. . ."

". . . and Mother yelled an angry word
you can't say when you're small.
But still my foot was fast asleep;
I'm guessing it was dreaming."

"I thought for sure it would wake up,
as loud as Mom was screaming.
Then Mother dropped her bowl of fruit
—two peaches and an orange. . ."

"and it. . .
um. . ."

Felled (verb): to cut or knock down

Ponce closed his eyes again. But this time, when they opened, they practically bugged out of his head. He developed a noticeable red tint and began rocking back and forth. The street was silent, except for the electric-buzz of the power lines above.

Then he fainted.

The two men holding Silky looked at each other. Without saying a word, they dropped him roughly to the dirty ground and retreated silently into the shadows.

Silky dance-sprinted toward me, and we both scampered up to the roof. As we bounded into the trees, I nearly stepped on a leaf gecko perched in the shadows.

Chapter 20: Open Eyes and Ears

We were high in the treetops of a park when I finally removed the duct tape from Silky's mouth.

I had thought seriously about leaving it on so I wouldn't have to hear him freak out.

When I removed the tape, Silky was unexpectedly calm. The first thing he said was, "Twenty thousand ariary? What were you thinking? That chameleon's pretty good. . ."

I laughed. "I don't have a single ariary in my pocket. I didn't know what else to do. I wasn't going to stand there and let you get beat up."

Silky paused. His newly–liberated mouth hung open in amazement. "Wow. That's wild. I mean, it's really dumb, but–wow–thanks!"

He put his headphones over his ears, and looked down at his convex feet. *"That unstylish chameleon out-rhymed me pretty badly."*

"Don't be silly! You're the reason we won that rhyme battle."

Silky looked confused.

"Let's just say that you aren't the only one to have had an unusual encounter tonight. It's a long story, but my new favorite saying is, 'Kids with open eyes and ears will be amazed at what appears.'"

Silky looked even more confused.

"With that duct tape on your mouth I knew I couldn't hear you, so as Ponce and I were battling, I kept looking over at you to make sure those goons hadn't taken you away—back into the shadows. At one point, a big crowd of people had gathered in front of you. I could barely see you. I was craning my neck trying to spot a flash of your orange shirt. I was thinking, 'orange, orange.' And that's when I remembered

---

Convex (adjective): shaped like the outside of a bowl: curving outward

that nothing in the English language rhymes with orange!"

Silky sat for a moment, processing. Then he jumped down out of the tree, smoothly ping–ponging from one branch to the next until he reached the ground. He looked up, smiled, and yelled, "Kids with open eyes and ears will be amazed at what appears."

For the first time in hours, Silky looked relaxed and confident. He took off his headphones and set out dance-walking, drawing inspiration from the sights, sounds, and smells of a warm, wet night in Madagascar's capital city.

Chapter 21: Tranquil

Lava slunk quietly to the window of Foosana's darkened motel room. Ambient electronic music played lightly inside.

Lava's natural movements were so sly and subtle that he often sneaked up on others without intending to do so. Given Foosana's rising temper, he was particularly worried about startling her tonight.

Foosana's instincts, however, were strong. She saw his silhouette against the moonlit sky and opened the window.

Lava RARELY entered through the door.

"Well, um. . . Greetings, Foosana. It was pretty, um, crazy out there tonight. The, um, fancy–pants silky lemur, um, nearly had, um, should we say, an, um, *accident*, tonight."

"*Nearly?*" Foosa replied, raising one eyebrow.

"He was, um, captured by some local, um, thugs, but. . . " Lava's voice fell. "Um, Oliver um, rescued him."

Foosana closed her eyes and took a long breath in through her snout. She held the breath for nearly twenty seconds before releasing it through her mouth, trying to expel the rapidly rising tension and frustration from her body.

Both Foosana and Lava see well in the dark, so the little leaf gecko was surprised–and briefly blinded–when Foosana opened the bathroom door, filling the room with bright light.

Foosana broke the silence, but not the tension, speaking in a cold and measured voice.

"Tomorrow is the finals. Lava. . . I need you to look inward and to. . . to. . . STOP FAILING!"

Veins bulged in her neck. She closed her eyes and took a deep, calming breath. She opened her eyes. *"Lava?"*

Lava–as leaf geckos are known to do when they feel threatened–had frozen with fear and turned the color of the table beneath him. He was practically invisible. . . until he waved his tail. Foosana continued.

"I want you, Lava, to sneak into the zookeeper's office in the Tana Zoo tonight and bring me some lemur tranquilizer. I assume you've heard of a tranquilizer, Lava. Tranquilizers are used to sedate animals–to make them fall asleep– so zookeepers and veterinarians can safely examine them.

"At contest time tomorrow night, I want to make sure Oliver is, should we say, safely examining the inside of his own eyelids." She paused again, and then her voice rose.

"I'M NOT, ahem. . ." Foosana started again. *"WE'RE NOT–going to drift back into obscurity while some silly rhyming lemur goes to Cape Town. IS THAT CLEAR?!"*

Chapter 22: Breakfast

I didn't bring up Ponce de Cammie–León at breakfast. That was Silky's story to tell. . . if he even wanted it told.

After twenty minutes, there was still no sign of Silky, so we ordered without him. I started to wonder if something else happened to him last night.

When the waiter finished taking our orders, Numbat was the first to bring "it" up, the proverbial giant baobab tree in the room. The three of us had avoided the topic since the second–round freak out.

"So, here's the mix on Silky. To understand him—both his crazy talent and his crazy total freak-outs—you've got to understand his story. Check out this article."

With that, Numbat handed us his iPad.

Proverbial (adjective): commonly spoken of or widely known

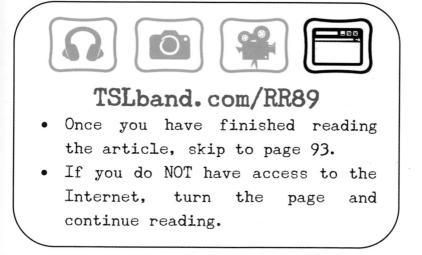

TSLband.com/RR89

- Once you have finished reading the article, skip to page 93.
- If you do NOT have access to the Internet, turn the page and continue reading.

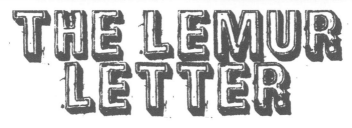

THE LEMUR LETTER

The Lemur Letter recently sat down with DJ, producer and musician Douglass "Silky" Sifaka for our "Gimme 5-Five Questions with a Celebrity" segment. Silky opened up about his childhood, his ear(s), and how we can all make a difference in the forests of Madagascar.

[1] **You are regarded as one of the top musicians in all of Madagascar. How did you get started with music?**

Silky: When I was only eighteen months old, my family and I were chased out of our home in Marojejy National Park by illegal loggers. We were then trapped by people catching lemurs for a zoo. The trappers took my parents and my sister, but one of them said to another that I was not cute enough for the zoo, so they let me go.

You would never believe it now, since I am very good looking and stylish today, but I was kind of awkward and funny looking when I was young.

Anyway, the experience with the trappers made me really sensitive about my appearance, and I became quiet and shy. Because of this shyness, I focused all of my free time on music as a kind of escape. Over the next few years, all this music practice turned me into an amazing musician. Now pretty much everybody likes me.

I am still skittish from having been chased by loggers and trapped by trappers. My doctor says I have Post Traumatic Stress Disorder, or PTSD.

The way the PTSD affects me—and it is different for everyone—is that I freak out when I am in danger. . . which is actually a lot, since, you know, I'm endangered.

[2] What is your greatest strength?

Silky: I have really good ears. They are really good looking ears, obviously. But more than that, they are really good ears for music. I have the ability to hear a musical note and immediately identify the note as a "C" or a "G" or whatever. That ability is called "perfect pitch." It helps me record music, play music, and sing along to music. I don't think I would be such an amazing musician without them.

[3] I can see why the prevention of illegal logging is such a big issue for you. Tell us a little about your work there.

Silky: I've been helping the Duke Lemur Center raise money to provide education in local villages around Marojejy. There are two key parts to the education. One is to help the locals understand that when they cut down forests in and around the park, they are destroying the lemurs' homes. But we also have to help the villagers find other ways to make money. Many villagers are cutting down the trees and selling the wood as a way to feed their families. The Duke Lemur Center is helping these tree cutters develop skills growing crops, or working in other jobs, so they can still support their families… without hurting the endangered lemurs. It won't happen overnight, but through supporting education, we can all help

Just then, Numbat grabbed the iPad back from me before I could finish reading.

"Hey Silky—how was your night? See any good bands?" Jenny Hart asked in her most friendly voice, when Silky dance–walked to our table.

Chapter 23: Captain Cage

"It was really good, and—hey—sorry about yesterday. I just kind of. . ."

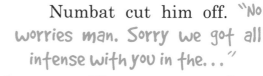

Numbat cut him off. "No worries man. Sorry we got all intense with you in the. . ."

The room was silent for a moment. Numbat was afraid to say the wrong thing. Silky, however, had already moved on and was thinking about his night.

"I had this crazy experience," Silky started. "I met a pirate. . ."

Then he paused to pull a neatly folded napkin from the back pocket of his bell-bottom pants. He began reading:

Captain Cage.
by Douglass "Silky" Sifaka

Last night I met a pirate.
Who had fallen on tough luck.
He'd tried to cross a busy street,
but his peg leg got stuck
inside an iron drainage guard
(a large and heavy grate)
he'd stepped in absent-mindedly
while he was ~~running~~ limping late.

I helped him out, he thanked me twice,
then said, "It's not my day.
The parrot I have had for years
just up and flew away.

I put some peanuts on my hat.
They are his favorite snack.
I hoped he would get hungry soon,
but he has not come back

"And lest you think a parrot
Would be easy to replace,
I'm telling you, I've shopped around,
and that is not the case!

"I've trapped and trained a pigeon now
but so far he's refrained
from sitting on my shoulder
in the way that he was trained.

"To show me he was not content
he gave my eye a scratch.
So now I have two injured eyes
that I will need to patch.

"And since that pigeon scratched my eye
I've found I'm not inclined
to keep him up there anyway
unless he is confined."

Perhaps his parrot will come back
Someday when he is older.
But until then he'll sail the sea,
caged pigeon on his shoulder.

When Silky finished we all clapped. Numbat blurted out, "Dude, where did THAT come from?"

Silky smiled. "Kids with open eyes and ears will be amazed at what appears."

I'm not sure if he'd actually met a pirate who was missing a parrot, but it didn't really matter. Silky had his groove back, and we loved it.

Chapter 24: Out Ordered

When my banana rice with bean cakes arrived, I knew I had been out—ordered. It was unusually spicy. I spent the whole meal wishing I had ordered the banana pot pie that the table next to us ordered. A slight breeze was blowing in the window, and the sweet smell of caramelized bananas wafted directly from their table to my lemur nose.

I finally couldn't take it anymore. I pulled my favorite fork from my pocket and, quietly, under the white tablecloth, telescoped it to full length. You see. . .

My favorite fork is four feet long,
and length–wise that is ample,
to reach the table next to me
and grab a little sample.

Chapter 25:
I Know a Guy Who Knows a Guy. . .

"I had an idea as I was out last night," Silky said between bites of fruit and leaves at breakfast. "When we present our poem in the finals, how rad would it be if we presented it as a really cool song with instruments and everything?"

"Cool idea," I said politely. "But the final round starts in a few hours. Where are we going to get instruments on a Sunday?"

Madagascar is one of those countries where most businesses are closed on Sunday.

Silky was one step ahead of me. "I know a guy who knows a guy who used to play bass for this dude's brother's band." We all stared at Silky, trying to keep up. "This dude's brother knows the owner of a music shop in town. I'll bet we could get him to loan us some instruments."

Before I could voice my opinion, a small potted plant fell from the railing next to us, shattering shards of red clay pot across our table. . . and all over what was left of my bean cakes.

Silky started to scream, but Jenny put her hand over his mouth.

We looked at the now-empty railing, but saw nothing.

"Haunted hotel?" Numbat joked.

"Hmm. . ." Jenny said suspiciously, as she stood up to take a closer look. She wiped her hand along the top of the railing before suddenly jumping back with a scream.

A well–camouflaged leaf gecko—who appeared to be as startled as Jenny —darted along the railing and out an open window.

"Was that..?"

It's hard to tell one leaf gecko from another, so we couldn't be sure this was Foosana's friend, Lava. Leaf geckos are common in Madagascar. It could have been a hungry gecko positioning to swoop our leftovers. Still, it fit a pattern of very suspicious behavior. Not to mention that half of my breakfast went to waste. . .

Chapter 26: Be Yourself

Silky and Jenny left directly from the restaurant to find "The Guy Who Knows a Guy Who Used to Play Bass for This Dude's Brother's Band."

After they left, Numbat got serious.

"Dude–you know–I get really nervous about the "improv" part of the gig. I'm kinda freaked out about, you know, not knowing what to say. Jenny–and you–always make up good stuff. I don't know if my brain works like that... you know?"

I know it's impolite to laugh when someone opens-up to you, but I almost couldn't help myself.

"Numbat, you always know the PERFECT thing to say! Remember that line yesterday about the 'south-end of a dog going north?' We were all pretty upset and you found a way to

Improv (verb): short for improvise; to make-up or invent on the spur of the moment

make us laugh. When you are just being yourself—just talking—you come up with all kinds of funny lines. You are creative and totally hilarious. That's part of why people love being friends with you."

I paused, wanting my final words to sink in. "When you get on stage, no rule states that you have to change or act a certain way, just because you are on a stage. Be yourself and do the funny things you do every day. People will laugh like crazy!"

After we talked, I went back to bed. I was really, REALLY sleepy. I didn't even wake up when...

Chapter 27: The Nap before the Storm

Bang!
. . .Boyoyoyoyoying

a pair of overloaded rickshaws crashed to a halt in front of our hotel.

Silky had indeed found "The Guy Who Knows a Guy Who Used to Play Bass for This Dude's Brother's Band," and "The Guy Who Knows a Guy Who Used to Play Bass for This Dude's Brother's Band" had indeed talked to his music–store–owning friend. That friend had indeed come through with a loan of instruments. . . though they weren't exactly what we had in mind.

The only things he had were instruments for a high school marching band. He also didn't have a truck to transport the gear.

So. . . Silky and Jenny convinced two rickshaw drivers to loan them their rickshaws for an hour to transport the instruments.

At 4:45 that afternoon, I woke up to Numbat jumping up and down on my bed and Silky using his skinny, hairy lemur hand to open one of my eyelids. Most lemurs don't hibernate, but I woke up still feeling like a bear in mid–winter.

I yawned and let out a yowl. Numbat continued jumping on my bed, so I croaked out, "Arright, arright. I'm getting up!" in a groggy, gravelly voice. Then I walked to the bathroom.

As soon as they left, I started to brush my teeth. I was too tired to stand, so I sat in a chair to let my electric toothbrush finish its work. I figured, "With an electric toothbrush, you don't really need to stand up to. . . "

Rickshaw (noun): a small hooded carriage with two wheels that is pulled by one person

Three seconds after I sat down in a chair, I fell back asleep. My electric toothbrush fell to the floor in front of me —running.

I was still sleeping in that chair—with my toothbrush still running on the floor—at 5:45pm when Jenny knocked on the door. The taxi was downstairs.

Jenny looked at my bloodshot eyeballs and heard my slightly slurred speech and sent Numbat running to fetch a doctor.

The doctor asked me a ton of questions that I barely remember answering. Then he called Jenny, Silky, and Numbat together right outside the door. He addressed the team in a hushed voice.

"It looks like he's been tranquilized. I won't know for sure without a blood test. It will take hours for the results to come back, but that's what the symptoms suggest."

He then gave me an intravenous infusion of medicine ("an IV") and wished us luck.

Intravenous (adjective): Existing or taking place within, or administered into, a vein or veins

This was a disaster—and completely consistent with the pattern of incidents over the last two days.

Chapter 28: Bailin' on Bean Cakes

I rode to the Rova with my head out the taxi window. The IV had helped me feel quite a bit better, but I was still groggy. I wanted as much fresh air as I could get. Everyone else was nervously quiet, until Numbat exploded into a monologue. He was so excited that he could barely get his words out in order.

"Dude!! I think Lava, like, actually saved you! I'll bet it went down like—like this. Lava sneaked some tranquilizer mix into your grub, right? Then when he was hanging out waiting for you to, you know, eat it, he accidentally busted the plant. Remember how you bailed on the last half of your bean cakes after the plant bomb? So, so, you probably only got half the mix. Right? You're going

Monologue (noun): a long uninterrupted speech

110

to be golden by the time this gig actually goes tonight!"

The idea may have been wishful thinking, but it encouraged us all. I WAS starting to feel a LITTLE more alert. . . though I was still pretty out of it.

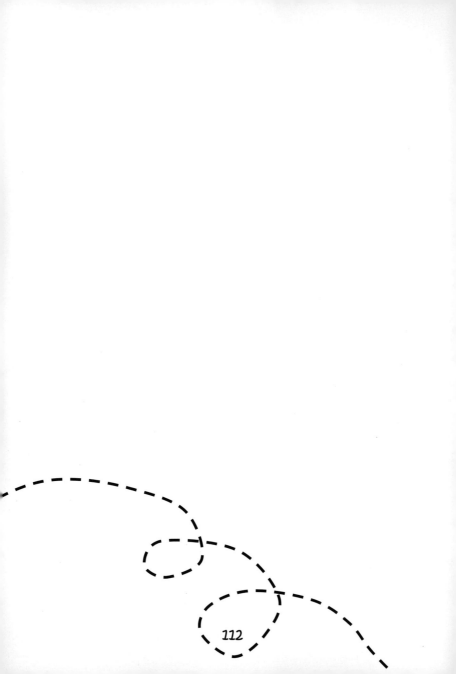

Chapter 29: Butterflies

"Wait, seriously?" Numbat whispered way too loudly. "The winning team gets an all-expense paid trip to another one of these in Cape Town?"

Parson was addressing the four remaining teams before the start of the final round. "THE RULES FOR THE FINALS ARE THE SAME AS FOR ROUNDS ONE AND TWO. THAT SAID, THERE IS ONE BIG DIFFERENCE BETWEEN TONIGHT AND THE FIRST TWO ROUNDS. THERE WILL BE A BIG CROWD. MAYBE 1,200 PEOPLE IN THE THEATER, AND THE PERFORMANCES ARE BEING BROADCAST LIVE ON RTM, MADAGASCAR'S LARGEST TV STATION."

Nearly everyone gasped when he said that. After a day of competing in front of *maybe* fifty people, this was going to be the big time. The skin beneath Silky's lemur hair got cold. A swarm of butterflies danced in Jenny's stomach.

"YOUR TOPIC FOR THE FINALS IS. . .

Chapter 30: Your Body

"Wait—my body, or your body? We all have different..."

The topic for the final round was "Your Body."

The team batted around ideas for nearly ten minutes without finding a bit of inspiration. My body was awake, but my mind was still in super–slow motion. We were stumped.

Numbat was getting frustrated. Jenny, who's ALWAYS positive, was getting worried. Silky was stressed. I paced around the room, my long ring tail dragging behind me. It bumped into tables and chairs at every turn. The room was silent.

Then Numbat broke wind.

Loudly.

Everyone chuckled, except for me. I was still staring into space, watching a fly as it buzzed around Numbat's hat.

"That's it!" I yelled. "I've got it."

They all looked at me.

"Even though a lot of people won't admit it, gas can be funny. That's true at almost any age. Let's write a poem about what happens when you eat something that does not, should we say, agree with you."

Silky gave me a knowing smile. He didn't say anything, but I knew we were thinking the same thing.

"Kids with open eyes and ears will be amazed at what appears."

Jenny picked up a pen and jumped into brainstorm mode. "What makes you—someone in general—gassy?"

The ideas came fast and furious. "Spicy foods" "Burritos" "Spicy wings."

Then, as if it were scripted, we all at once said, **"Beans!"**

With that, we were off and running. We'd soon created the outline, rhyme scheme, and meter for a beans story. Jenny and I sat down at one end of the table to turn it into a full poem. Numbat always travels with a small Martin practice guitar, and he and Silky began to create a song.

With twenty-five minutes to spare, we'd created a poem called "Bad Bean Defect." With fifteen minutes left, we'd turned it into a song.

BAD BEAN DEFECT
By Mister Lemur

After snacking on beans
I began to suspect,
that these beans contained some
kind of bad bean defect.

My stomach expanded,
my eyes got quite wide.
It felt like a hot spring
was gurgling inside

my belly, my gut,
or whatever you'd call it.
It's about to explode,
and I'd like to forestall it.

This pain is not normal,
and please understand,
it feels like I've swallowed
a whole marching band.

They're playing four trumpets,
two horns, a trombone,
and the band leader's shouting
through his megaphone.

They marched past my kidney
to my large intestine,
if you know how to silence them,
yell the suggestion!

My mom called the doc
who said, "Give him some Tums.
That should help silence
the horns and the drums."

And the doctor was right,
and the band went on break
and my stomach returned
to just a dull ache.

So surely by now
you must know what this means. . .
next time I am hungry. . .
I won't eat three cans of beans!

"We've got five minutes, let's rehearse it one more time," I yelled, after we finished another pass through the song.

Silky pulled out a recorder. "Let's track this one—for when they do a TV special about us winning!"

TSLband.com/RR119

As we ran down the hall to submit our poem, I could feel the excitement building inside of me. We had a great poem and an even better song. There was no doubt we were going to win. I pictured our team visiting Table Rock in Cape Town before the next round. I laughed a big, happy—and wide awake—lemur laugh.

Chapter 31: The Finals

When all four finalists had submitted their stories, Parson began leading the teams along the familiar path back to the presentation stage in Arts and Culture Building. Right before he walked into the door of that building, he stopped and turned to face us. A mini bus screeched to a stop beside us.

"THE FINALS" he smiled, **"WILL BE IN THE MAIN OPERA HOUSE!"** He shouted the final three words for effect.

"Whoa!" I thought. "That won't do anything to calm my nerves!"

As we rode in the bus, I closed my eyes, took three deep breaths, and visualized myself on stage. It calmed me. Foosana's team rode in silence. They displayed very little emotion, though I did once catch Foosana looking at Lava with a smile that said, "We have a secret."

That worried me.

The bus rounded one final banked turn and the opera house came into view.

"Dude!" Numbat exclaimed. "Check out all those people!"

A huge crowd was milling around a throng of rickshaws, taxis, and men selling bottled water.

Local TV station RTM had a van parked in front. A reporter was interviewing people in line waiting to get inside.

We followed Parson through a side door and into the backstage area. Parson gave us a quick tour of the Opera House. Each team was assigned its own dressing room, which I thought was pretty cool.

We were able to peek into the crowd with no one noticing. Big, yellowish light bulbs hung from the ceiling above the theater–style rows of seats. Those seats were nearly full, and the crowd was already making a lot of noise.

We drew numbers from a hat to determine the presentation order. We were last. That meant we'd know the score to beat... but we'd have to wait—nervously—through each of the other team's presentations.

Foosana's team went first. They did a song.

We couldn't really hear the song clearly from our dressing room, but the thunderous response from the crowd told us she had probably scored well. I looked at Silky, but he was calm and confident.

If Numbat was nervous, he didn't let it show. "Ha! Maybe they're cheering 'cause she fell off the stage!"

I loved how loose and confident they were. I wished I were as relaxed.

We were able to hear a recording later.

Then they burst into song. It was a catchy, dance-pop tune called "Cell City." I had to admit it was pretty awesome.

TSLband. com/RR123

Chapter 32: You're On!

We waited through two more performances. Each of these earned much smaller ovations.

Then Tambo stuck his bushy white beard between the red velvet curtains. "Scheming Lemurs, you're on in five minutes."

The curtains closed and the show went to commercial. The roadies quickly carried the already–tuned instruments to the stage. Back in our dressing room, I closed my eyes and visualized playing my bass guitar part. Numbat paced. Jenny stretched. Silky bobbed his head, eyes closed, singing to himself.

TSLband.com/RR125

- Once you have finished watching the video, skip to page 136.
- If you do NOT have access to the Internet, turn the page and continue reading.

Chapter 33: Body Band (Print Version)

Tambo stuck his head through the curtains again. "Scheming Lemurs, you're on in one minute."

In a darkened backstage hallway, a shadowy figure laughed, *"When their instruments turn up missing, Tambo and the judges will have to let us perform in the next round instead!"* Then she laughed as she pushed an overflowing wheelbarrow—with all of our borrowed instruments—out a side door and into the back of a waiting truck.

Only then did the shadowy figure remove her disguise. The truck sped away, taking our instruments, and our chances of advancing, off into the night. Foosana slunk back to her dressing room. She wasn't proud of cheating, but she was elated by the thought that nothing else stood between her and Cape Town.

Tambo peeked into The Scheming Lemurs' dressing room a final time. "Ok, you're on!"

Jenny Hart smiled a big, excited smile. "Places everybody. Let's do this!"

The curtain opened, the lights came up, and we stepped to the stage. It took my eyes a moment to adjust to the brightness. Then they began darting back and forth. A terrified look came over my face. Wait! Was this possible? All of our gear was. . . gone!

Silky was the first to speak up. . . and freak out. *"Aaah! Somebody took our gear! Aaaaggghhhh!"*

Jenny looked dejected. "Oohh, the fans will be so disappointed. . . "

My brain tried to rationalize what was happening. "I do not see how this can be. It does not make much sense to me!"

As Silky was freaking out, and Jenny and I were feeling sorry for ourselves, Numbat strode forward and said, "Don't worry, dudes. I totally got this. Just be cool and do what I do."

Despite all his stage fright and fear of improvising, he calmly and confidently looked at the rest of us. . . and started making body noises.

"Pop!" "Shh"
"Hiccup!" "Cough"

The audience response ranged from blank stares to confused looks.

Silky, Jenny and I joined him, adding whatever body noises we could think of. We couldn't help but laugh as this odd collection of body noises began to resemble—and then was— a beat.

Numbat began making up a song, improvising on the spot.

Come and join the Body Band,
we're making up a song.
Unless you've got no body
this is how you play along.

You say you have no instrument?
I don't think you understand.
'Cause if you've got a body,
you are in the Body Band!

Hiccup through a poster tube,
cough low to add some bass.
Buzz like you're a bumblebee
while you contort your face.

You say you have no instrument?
I don't think you understand.
'Cause if you've got a body,
you are in the Body Band!

Breathe like you've just run a mile.
Snore like a lumberjack.
Howl as though you are a wolf
that just stepped on a tack.

You say you have no instrument?
I don't think you understand.
'Cause if you've got a body,
you are in the Body Band!

People loved it! A few even ran on stage to make noise and dance.

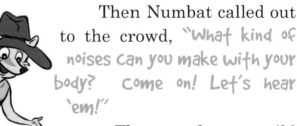

Then Numbat called out to the crowd, "What kind of noises can you make with your body? Come on! Let's hear 'em!"

The crowd went wild with the sounds of snaps and claps and burps and chirps and whistles and just about any other body noise you could imagine.

Foosana heard the crowd noise from her dressing room backstage and ran to a side door. Lava was perched on her shoulder. She gazed at the stage in disbelief.

With the audience participation "bridge" complete, Numbat resumed singing.

> Make a drum beat on your thighs.
> Tick—tock like you're a clock.
> In this symphony we all can be
> Johann Sebastian Bach.
>
> You say you have no instrument?
> I don't think you understand.
> 'Cause if you've got a body,
> you are in the Body Band!

Pull a finger, pop a cheek.
Click your heels in time.
Take that quarter in your shorts
and rub it against a dime.

You say you have no instrument?
I don't think you understand.
'Cause if you've got a body,
you are in the Body Band!

You say you have no instrument?
I don't think you understand.
'Cause if you've got a body,
you are in the Body Band!

We laughed like crazy when it was over,
but no one laughed louder than Numbat.

Chapter 34: Be Yourself and People Will Laugh

As we exchanged high fives backstage, Numbat looked happier than I'd ever seen him.

Silky was the first to ask the question we were all wondering. "Did you really just make that up on the spot? It was amazing!"

"Yeah, Dude! For real! Check this! As. . ." Numbat looked at me, and then continued, "as a wise man once told me, 'You don't have to change just 'cause you're on a stage. Be yourself, and people will laugh—with you—like crazy.'"

Improvising Body Band was a big deal for him on a lot of levels. I don't think I've ever been happier for anyone.

Chapter 35: And the Winner is. . .

We, along with the other teams, were seated in the front row as Parson stepped forward to the microphone. Just like the Academy Awards, cameramen surrounded us like flies. The fourth place team was announced, then the third place team. That left us, and Miss Foosa.

Parson continued. "JUST **TWO TEAMS** REMAIN. TWO TEAMS THAT PUT ON DELIGHTFUL MUSICAL SHOWS TONIGHT. BUT THERE CAN ONLY BE ONE CHAMPION OF RIVALS IN RHYME MADAGASCAR. AS YOU KNOW, THAT CHAMPION WILL RECEIVE AN ALL-EXPENSE PAID TRIP TO CAPE TOWN, SOUTH AFRICA. THERE, THEY WILL COMPETE AGAINST TEAMS FROM ALL OVER AFRICA FOR THE RIGHT TO BE CALLED THE CONTINENT CHAMPION. THAT CONTINENT CHAMPION WILL THEN ADVANCE TO THE HEMISPHERE FINALS IN SYDNEY, AUSTRALIA. (At this, the crowd cheered excitedly.)

"I wish I felt better about this," I whispered. We had explained to the judges that our instruments had been stolen and asked them not to disqualify us for presenting a different poem than we'd submitted. We were one of two teams left, so we hadn't been disqualified, but they still might dock us points. And Foosana's song WAS really good.

"AND NOW, WITHOUT FURTHER DELAY. . . THE CHAMPION OF THIS YEAR'S RIVALS IN RHYME MADAGASCAR IS. . .

"MISS FOOSA!"

The crowd erupted with cheers. I groaned and clapped half-heartedly. Silky sank in his chair, wrapping his white tail around his face, covering his eyes. Numbat instinctively curled into a ball beneath his seat.

Parson continued, "FOOSANA AND HER TEAM WERE CONSISTENTLY EXCELLENT THROUGH ALL THREE ROUNDS.

AS THE CHAMPIONS, THEY WILL RECEIVE AN ALL-EXPENSE PAID TRIP TO CAPE TOWN, SOUTH AFRICA TO REPRESENT MADAGASCAR IN THE AFRICA FINALS. WE KNOW THEY WILL MAKE US PROUD. LET'S GIVE THEM ANOTHER BIG ROUND OF APPLAUSE."

I cheered half-heartedly again.

"AND LET'S GIVE A BIG ROUND OF APPLAUSE AS WELL TO OUR RUNNERS UP-OUR SECOND PLACE FINISHERS-WHO WERE VERY ENTERTAINING IN THEIR OWN RIGHT. . . "MISTER LEMUR AND THE SCHEMING LEMURS!"

I was later told that the crowd gave us a hardy ovation, but I was too distraught to notice.

Parson resumed speaking, "ALTHOUGH OUR RUNNER-UP WILL NOT RECEIVE AN ALL-EXPENSE-PAID TRIP, BECAUSE THEY ARE THE SECOND-PLACE FINISHER, THEY WILL ALSO BE INVITED TO PARTICIPATE IN THE NEXT ROUND IN CAPE TOWN. WE HOPE THEY WILL BE ABLE TO GO AND ALSO REPRESENT MADAGASCAR. LET'S GIVE THEM ONE MORE BIG HAND!"

I felt Jenny's hand on my shoulder, shaking me.

"Did you hear that? We still get to go!"

Chapter 36: Jobs

We left Tana on a train toward Antsirabe. Each of us sat quietly, looking out the window as the outlines of houses and barns flew past in the darkness. The rhythmic clacking of the train wheels lulled us toward sleep. What an exhausting weekend.

Jenny Hart finally spoke, giving off positive energy as always. "Look. . . I know we're all bummed that we didn't finish in first place, but look at what we overcame. We feel cheated, but look at what is in front of us! We still get to go to Cape Town!"

Antsirabe (noun): A city between Tana and Ranomafana.

"Dude, we need to get J.O.B.S." Numbat interjected. "Between paying for the stolen gear and getting to Cape Town, we're going to need a fat stack of cash."

"Don't–don't look at me." Silky stammered, his tired, red eyes clashing unfashionably with his bright orange sunglasses. "I've already got a job. How do you think I pay for my amazing wardrobe?"

We again became silent. Then it hit me. It was so obvious.

"Hey! I know what we can do! Let's form a band! Our Bad Bean song was—I mean, is—awesome! Let's write more songs, record an album, and go on tour. We can make money to pay for the instruments and the trip. Plus, it would be pretty cool to be in a band! Right?"

We all agreed that it sounded like a reasonable idea. We decided to get together the following Thursday at The VBC to talk about it. For now, though, everyone else wanted to sleep.

I, however, was suddenly way too excited to sleep. I continued chattering, unloading a stream of conscious flow of plans and thoughts about the band on Numbat.

"Dude," he finally interjected, "this is not the time or place for this train of thought." Then he put on headphones and pretended to sleep.

I stared out the window in silence for a few moments. The Writing Fly's words echoed in my head. *Kids with open eyes and ears will be amazed at what appears.*

I pulled my pocket journal from my pocket and began to write.

Come and ride the Train of Thought,
it doesn't matter where. . .

~ The End ~

About the Author

Oliver *"Mister"* Lemur is a ring-tailed lemur. He moved to Madagascar's Ranomafana National Park when he was very young. He lives there with his parents, his sister, "Pup," and his dog Henry. Oliver attends Namorana Elementary School, and plays the bass guitar. In addition to his native Lemur language, Oliver speaks English and French.

Oliver journals regularly and the notes from his journal (and his friends' journals) played a key role in his retelling of this adventure. This is book one in The Scheming Lemurs series.

OTHER WORKS

BOOKS

MISTER LEMUR'S TRAIN OF THOUGHT
Gold Medal for Children's Poetry, 2011 Moonbeam Awards
(a collection of 66 of Mister Lemur's rhymes). Grades 2-5

IT WILL TAKE A LOT OF US TO LIFT A HIPPOPOTAMUS (32 pages). Grades Pk – 2

THE SANTA CLAUS ALARM (by Lemur Pup)
(32 pages). Grades Pk – 2 (by Mister Lemur's little sister)

MUSIC

Adventures in Your Head (music album)

Adventures in Writing Camp: You Won't Believe Where Writing Will Take You!

Adventures in Writing Camp: What Could Be Better?

All books and music can be purchased at
www.TheLemurStore.com. A portion of sales is
donated to causes supporting the protection of
lemurs and/or lemur habitat.

Hans and Jen Hartvickson have been creating stories and music together since 2010. They chose "Mister Lemur" as their pen-name after falling in love with lemurs during a trip to Madagascar.

Hans and Jen were inspired to write by their mothers, who are both retired teachers. They are blessed to work with a wonderful team of musicians, artists, teachers and friends to bring Mister Lemur to the world. They spend their summers helping elementary school students become authors at Mister Lemur's Adventures in Writing Camp. www.AIWcamp.com.

Hans has been writing since the first grade. He loves sharing the fun of rhyming stories with kids of all ages. Hans holds a bachelor's degree in Economics from Stanford University and an M.B.A. from The University of Pennsylvania's Wharton School.

Jen travels the country speaking to schools, art associations and after school programs about the importance of writing, setting goals, and making plans. She earned a bachelor's degree in Sociology and a master's degree in Education from Stanford University.